W9-BDJ-697

The Berenstain Bears' EASTER SURPRISE

 Published by Scholastic Inc.
CARTWHEEL BOOKS and the CARTWHEEL BOOKS logo
are trademarks and/or registered trademarks of Scholastic Inc.

Library of Congress Cataloging-in-Publication Data

Berenstain, Stan
The Berenstain Bears' Easter surprise / Stan & Jan Berenstain.
p. cm.
"Cartwheel books."
Summary: As the Berenstain Bears prepare to celebrate Easter, Papa, Mama, and Brother reminisce about another Easter when Brother was given a very special surprise.
ISBN 0-590-94730-3
[1. Babies—Fiction. 2. Easter—Fiction. 3. Brothers and sisters—Fiction. 4. Bears—Fiction.] I. Berenstain, Jan. II. Title.
PZ7.B4483Benbg 1998
[E]—dc21 97-33301
CIP
AC

10 9 8 7 6 5 4 3 2 1 8 9/9 0/0 01 02

Printed in the U.S.A. 37
First printing, March 1998

The Berenstain Bears'
EASTER SURPRISE

Stan & Jan Berenstain

SCHOLASTIC INC.
New York Toronto London Auckland Sydney

Bear Country, friends,
as any observer can plainly see,
is a really and truly
fine place to be,

especially for cubs
and other small fry.

Baby robins
learning to fly,
young frogs and bunnies
learning to hop.

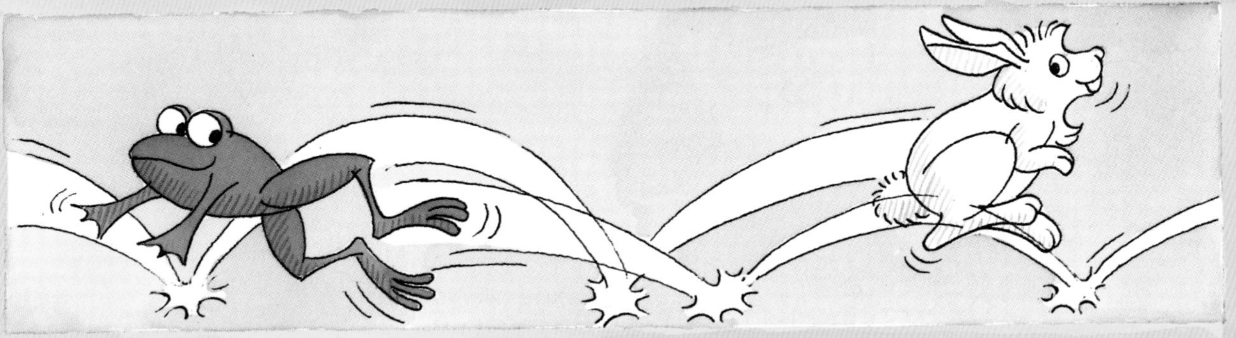

All ***kinds*** of young 'uns,
and every spring season
another new crop,

except that one Easter time
when the cycle of seasons
came to a screeching,
grinding, sudden stop!

So, friends, let us now
turn back the clock
to before Sister was born

and Brother was the only
cub on the block;

to when the Bears' tree house wasn't nearly so grand;

when a very strange thing occurred in Bear land.

No one really
knows the cause—
a shift, perhaps,
in the natural laws,
some unfortunate bit
of cosmic bad luck—
but somehow that winter,
the seasons got stuck!
What happened to spring?
Where did it go?
And Easter?
What about Easter?
Had it all been called off
on account of the snow?

Now in the fall of that winter
when the seasons got stuck,
Bear Country was having
very ***good*** weather luck.

"Dear," called Mama,
"Papa forgot his lunch today."
So lunch in hand,
Brother Bear was on his way.

Woodsbear Papa
was off in the wood
chopping, chopping
as only he could.

Yes, as any observer
can plainly see,
Bear Country was
a great place to be—
a great place to spend
your growing-up time.

There were puddles to jump,

trees to climb.

Plants that catch flies,
grasses that whistle,
the lesson you learn
backing into a thistle.
OUCH!

So much to do
and see and know,
a wonderful place
in which to grow,
but...and here's the rub,
a little lonesome
for an only cub.

Oh, Brother had friends—
the gang who hung 'round
down by the bog.
There was Bill Bunny
and Finerty Frog,
whose idea of excitement
was sunning himself
on an old rotting log.

And there wasn't very much
on Fred Firefly's mind,
but working the switch
on his electric behind.

As for Bill Bunny,
there just was no stopping
his rabbity habit
of hippity-hopping.

But when he reached
Papa's workplace,
a question arose;
it was as plain as the face
on Papa Bear's nose.
A curious cub,
he made full use
of his ears and eyes.
That Brother had questions
was no surprise.
He had enough, in fact,
for three cubs his size.

"I have a question,"
said Brother to Dad.
"Ask it," said Pa.
"Don't stammer, my lad."
"W-well," stammered Brother—
"my question, Dad..."
"Go ahead and ask it!
Don't stand there
hemming and hawing."
"Tell me," said Brother,
***"why are you standing
on that limb you are sawing?"***

"A good question," said Pa.
"Do you have any more?
It's one of the things
Papas are for."

"I have many," said Brother.
"There's so much to know.
Like where do we come from?
Like where do we go?

"What makes the sun shine?
Why do rivers flow?
In the middle of a river,
how deep does it get?
Do fishes get thirsty?
Why is water wet?
Where does your lap go
when you stand up?
How many fluid ounces
in a buttercup?"

"Yes, you may ask me any question
no matter how far out.

Being open to questions
is what parenting's about.
I have all the answers.
The who, what, why, and where.
Just as sure as my name is
...Barb Q. Pop, er,
Parpa Q. Bop...
Garba Pew..."

Brother kept asking questions
as the season progressed.
In fact, he became
a bit of a pest.

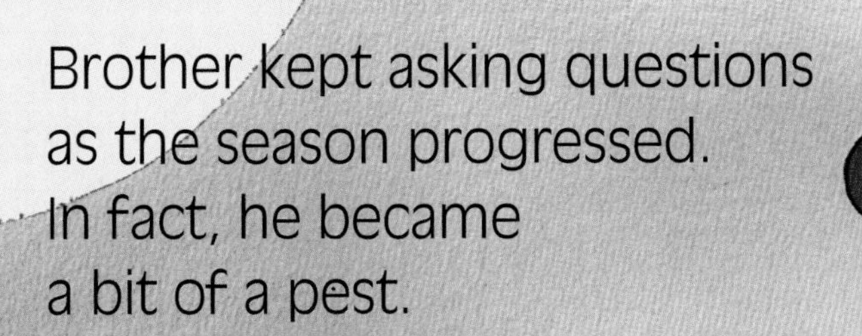

But whatever the season,
Bear Country was fun,
though it was
still a bit lonesome
being Mama and Papa's
only small son.
As for the gang
down by the bog —
Bill Bunny and Fred
and Finerty Frog —
well, as the old saying goes,
when fair weather ends,
you can say good-bye
to fair-weather friends.
Only Bill Bunny came venturing out
to see what winter
was all about.

It was a strange sort of winter—
gloomy and gray.
And, somehow, it seemed
to have come to stay.

"Hmm," said Papa.
"Something's gone wrong.
This winter is hanging on
much, much too long."

He looked at the papers,
turned on the TV,

checked every reference
book in the tree.

"Something's gone very wrong.
It's more than bad luck.
Somehow or other,
the seasons got stuck."

"But that cannot be!"
said Mama Bear.
"Maybe not," said Papa.
"But just look out there."
Ma looked out of the window
of their home sweet tree.
There was a whiteout as far
as the eye could see.

"But what about spring?
And Easter?
What about Easter?"

"Easter? What's Easter?"
asked small Brother Bear.
"What's Easter? It's a day
of treats!" said Papa Bear.

"It's delicious tastes,
yummy smells,

"coconut eggs
with chocolate shells.

Colored eggs
in paper grass,
treats for every
lad and lass.

Rainbow colored
jelly beans—
reds and yellows,
blues and greens.
Sweets and treats
of every kind—
there's no telling
what you may find.

Molasses, mocha,
treacle, honey.
And best of all—

the EASTER BUNNY!"

"Now, Papa," said Mama,
"if you please,
you can't see the forest
for the trees.

And while I don't deny
those things are fun,
Easter means much more,
my son.

It's a new beginning,
the warm sun melting
snow and ice,
bringing forth crocus,
tulips, edelweiss.

"Drawing new life
from the cold winter earth,
baby robins,
the miracle of birth.

The great rainbow
after a warm spring rain."

"What's a miracle?" asked Brother.
"Son, it's something wonderful
we can't quite explain.

And this Easter," said Mama,
looking into Brother's eyes,

"you'll have
an extra-special
Easter surprise."

And at that very moment,
Brother slipped off
Mama's lap.
Hmm? Was Mama's lap
getting smaller?
Or was it just that Brother
was getting taller?
Or even a little
of both perhaps —
which is often the way
with cubs and laps.

"Come!" said Pa.
"It's time for Boss Bunny
to wiggle his ears."

It has been the custom
for years and years
for Boss Bunny to signal spring
by wiggling his ears.

"We can count on Boss Bunny.
He wouldn't let anything
happen to spring.
And certainly not Easter—
Easter's his ***thing!***"

Not a sign of Boss Bunny,
not a wiggle or whit,
except a small one saying...
Boss Bunny has quit!

Boss just couldn't do this!
Had he no pride?
"What about spring?
And Easter?" they cried.

"And...and...and...,"
said Brother,
with tears in his eyes,
"wha-what about
my Easter surprise?"

Pa was especially
down in the mouth.
"Who will bring
our jelly beans—
our reds and yellows,
blues and greens?"

"And my surprise,"
said Brother,
"what might it have been?
A giant Easter egg
in a decorated tin?
A basket of yellow
marshmallow chicks?
A lifetime supply
of lemon sticks?"

Mama just smiled
and gave a small shrug,
reached down and gave Brother
a Mama Bear hug.

Said Pa, "There must be a way
of changing our luck,
of saving Easter and getting
the seasons unstuck."

And at that very moment
of despair and desperation,
Papa Bear was struck
by a full-fledged inspiration.
"Say...talk about
your Easter surprise,
just try this one
on for size!"

"Yes, I'll be the Easter Bunny.
I can do it, my dears.
The first thing I'll need
is slightly bigger ears.
Then some nice long whiskers.
These broom straws will do—
fasten them on
with bunny whisker glue.
Now let's twitch my whiskers,
train my ears to flop,
and now a bit of practice
on my bunny hop hop hop."

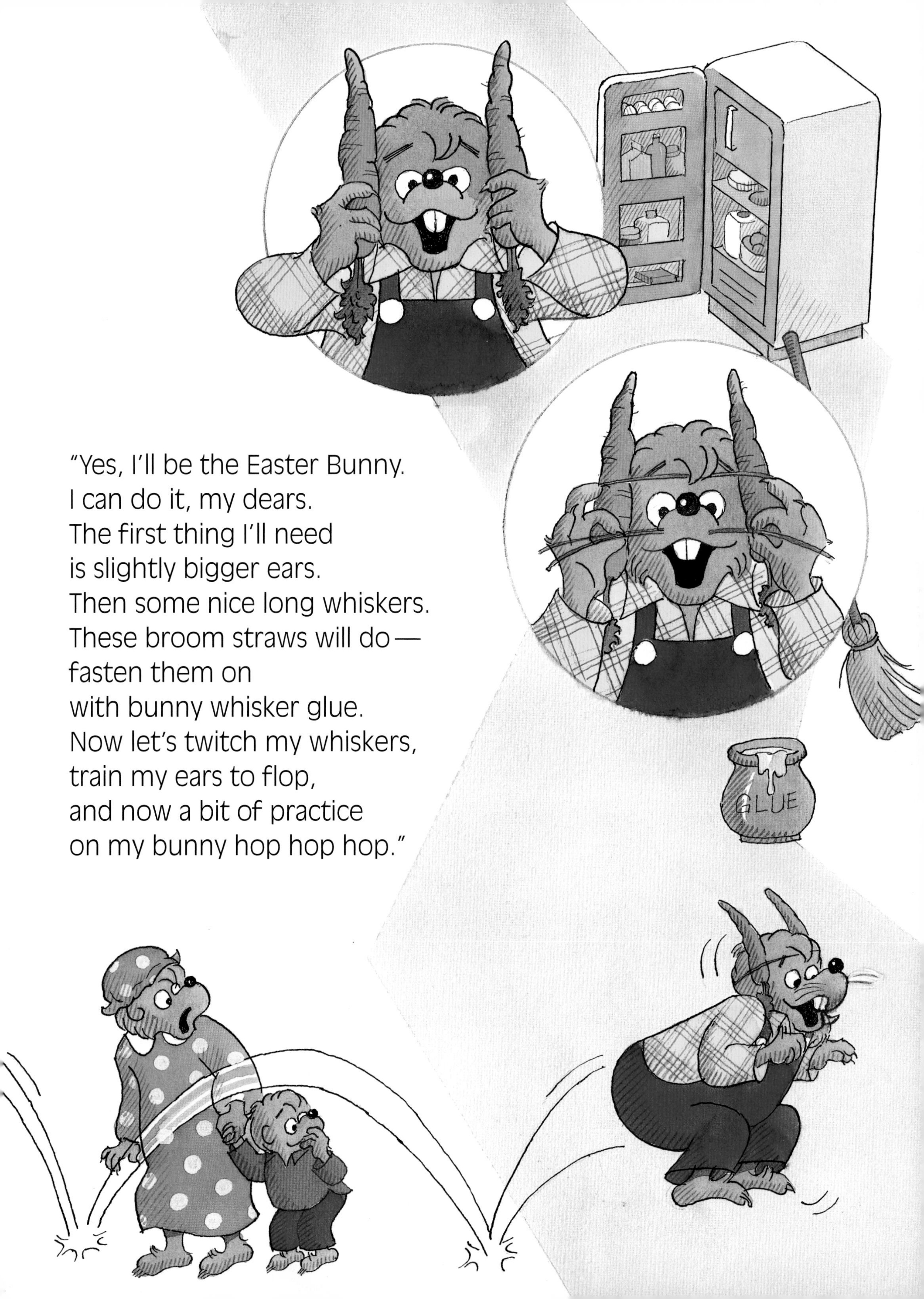

"The next thing we'll need
is a ready egg supply,
six or seven packets
of Easter egg dye;

some practical arrangement
of scrap lumber and planks
to direct the egg
supply into the mixing tanks.

"Then an extra nail or two
and one more rubber band.
Now, this last connection—
here, son, give me a hand.
Now all that's left to do,
as you can plainly see,
is hook the thing up
to my good old model-T."
It's working!
It's working!

It’s not working!
It’s not working!

There was much on the mind
of small Brother Bear.
As he pondered the questions
of who, what, and where,
who should come hopping
over the hill
but Brother Bear's friend,
Bunny Bill.

Now it was Bill
who wanted to play.
"Hi, there," said Bill.
"Wanna play?"

"Sorry," said Brother,
"I just can't today.
I've got too much
on my mind.
And there's somebody very special
that I simply have to find."

"Somebody special," said Billy.
"Who's that, Brother Bear?"

"The boss of all the bunnies —
the one and only Easter hare!"

Then Bill said something
that caused
Brother's jaw to drop.
"No problem, come with me,
Boss Bunny is my pop."

"Wow!" said Brother Bear.
"What a piece of luck!
He can help save Easter
and get the seasons unstuck!"

Then Bill led Brother
through a secret trapdoor
that no bear
had ever entered before.

It led to a secret
underground room!
It was dark and deserted
and quiet as a tomb,

except for some mice,
a bushy-tailed example
of genus ***catus catus***,
and Boss Bunny's
vast collection
of Easter apparatus.

There was a great
assembly line
of fabulous machines
capable of making
ten million jelly beans.
And Boss Bunny's
big claim to fame—
a device that could write
any cub's name.

Just up ahead
was a funny little door
with a narrow crack of light
showing at the floor.

In a room behind the door,
reclining on a shelf
was the erstwhile Easter Bunny,
Boss Bunny himself.

"Huh? Wha? All right, Sonny,
state your business,
spit it out.
What's this intrusion
all about?"

"Please, sir," said Brother,
"there's no need to shout.
But Easter and spring
is what it's all about!"

"Easter and spring?
Who cares about Easter?
And spring is a bore.

"Do you have any idea
of just how long
I've managed Easter
and kept the seasons
moving along?

Twitching my whiskers,
wiggling my ears.
Why, it's undignified
for someone
of my golden years!

Do you have any idea
of what it means
to make ten million
jelly beans?

The paperwork,
the regulations,
the egg supply,
the aggravations—
not to mention the aches
and pains.

I've got arthritis, bursitis,
mixer elbow, sinusitus.
I'm old and crabby,
bent and stooped."

"But, please!" said Brother.
"No Easter and spring?
Why, that would ruin
everything!"

"Look!" said Boss,
"I'll say it again.
Who cares about Easter?
And spring is a bore!
I'm fed up to here
and I'm not going
to take it anymore."

But Mr. Bunny, we *need* Easter and spring! We *need* a warm sun melting snow and ice.
All that Easter hocus-pocus 'bout daffodils and crocus
Tulips! Crocus!

starts my body achin'
and my teeth a'hurtin'.
Edelweiss!
So stop your beggin'
and your blurtin'.
My decision to resign
is absolutely
firm and certain.
Drawing new life
from the cold winter earth,
baby robins,
the miracle of birth.
Not going to take it anymore.
Not going to take it anymore.

Some of that rainbow
got through to Boss Bunny.
The great spring rainbow's
lovely light
touched his heart
and set things right.
It straightened his back,
it loosened his joints,
it reduced his aches and pains
by ten percentage points.

His ears began to wiggle,
his whiskers began to twitch.
Then Boss Bunny reached around
and pulled the master switch!

All right you bunnies,
it's Easter time.
So hop to it!
Get back on the job...
and DO IT!

On Easter morning
Brother opened his eyes,
stretched and remembered
his Easter surprise.

"Come in here!" called Mama.
"There's something you must see!"
Marshmallow chicks! thought Brother.
A chocolate egg and bunny!
In fact, it was all three!

What was in the basket
was a baby!
A little baby bear!
Brother Bear was so surprised,
all he did was stare.

Then as he reached to touch
her tiny toes,
her small fist accidentally
popped him on the nose.

"Say! For a tiny baby,
she has quite a punch!"
And as he rubbed his nose,
he knew—it was more
than just a hunch—

that something wonderful had happened;
that he wouldn't be lonesome anymore;
that his extra-special Easter surprise
had been well worth waiting for!

"Papa," he said, "I have one question."
"You may ask me any question,"
said Papa Bear to Brother.

"The baby?
Where did the baby come from?"
"Hmmm," said Pa,
"I think that one's for your mother."

"Remember about robins?" said Ma.
"And the miracle of birth?"
"Mama! You got your lap back!"
interrupted Brother...

and Mama had!

• About the Authors •

Stan and Jan Berenstain have been writing and illustrating books about bears for more than thirty years. In 1962, their self-proclaimed "mom and pop operation" began producing one of the most popular children's book series of all time — ***The Berenstain Bears***. Since then, children the world over have followed Mama Bear, Papa Bear, Sister Bear, and Brother Bear on over 100 adventures through books, cassettes, and animated television specials.

Stan and Jan Berenstain live in Bucks County, Pennsylvania. They have two sons, Michael and Leo, and four grandchildren.

DATE			
2/98			B 1095